I0784052

Ocean's Daughter

JANET SIERZANT

Ocean's Daughter
Copyright © 2018 Janet Sierzant
ISBN: 978-0-9916067-8-8

Back Cover Photo : Brian Donnelly

La Maison Publishing, Inc.
Vero Beach, Florida
The Hibiscus City
lamaisonpublishing@gmail.com

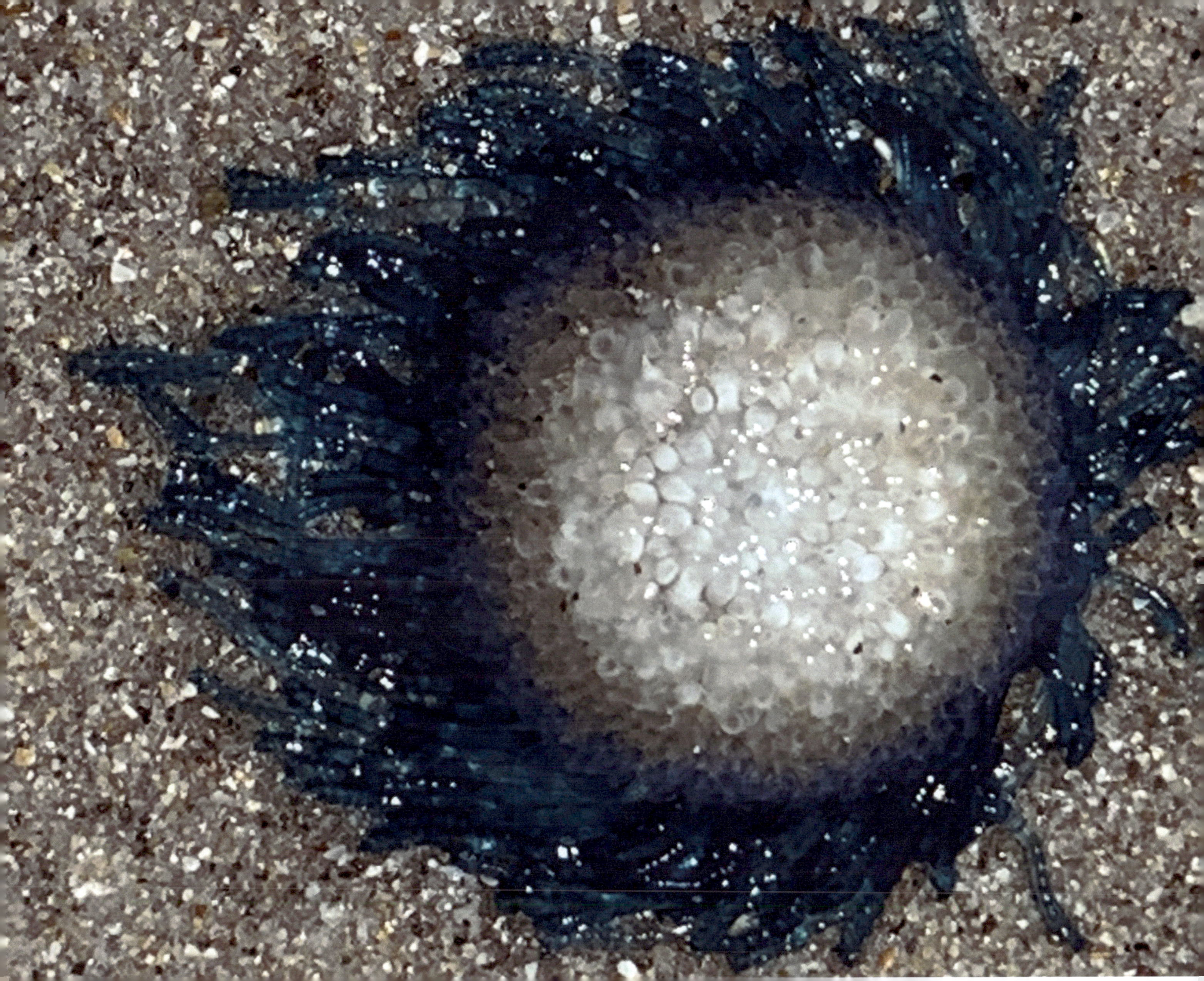

OCEAN
SPEED LIMIT
25

Turtle Trax

Presented by the Mental Health Association in Indian River County to promote awareness to those who suffer from mental illness.

Hibiscus Honey
Heritage Center

Faux Nesta
20th Street & 14th Avenue

East Meets West
J.C. Park

Inturlenational
Sexton Plaza

Flora Bella
Riverside Park

Very Vero
City Hall

Freedom- Liberty
Indian River County

Goldie
Mental Health Association

Peace on Earth
Royal Palm Point

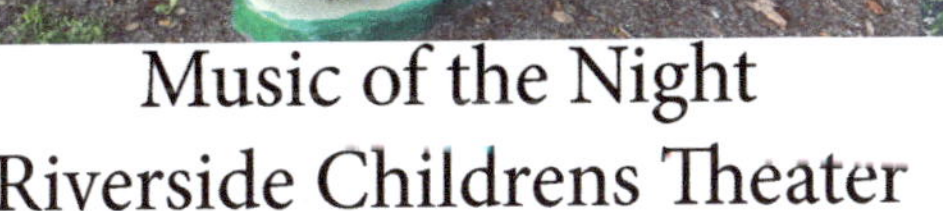

Peace on Earth
Back

Music of the Night
Riverside Childrens Theater

Born in the USA
Sea Turtle Inn

Legal Loggerhead
Rossway Swan Law

Indian River
Mall

Monet's Garden
Vero Beach Library

Florida Scene
Indian River Medical

Ridley
Rock City Gardens

Ethel
Environmental Learning

Vero Beach
High School

Stormy
Rescue Station 11

Erma
Indian River Medical

Shelter
Habitat for Humanity

Recycling Rosie
Sebastian Elementary

Turtleda
VB Chamber of Commerce

| Turtle Safari | Florida Flo | See Turtle | Ed |
| Humiston Park | Hospice House | VB Chamber of Commerce | Ocean Club |

| Shelter | Captain Carl Caretta | Neptune | Endless Summer |
| Habitat for Humanity | The Moorings | Mental Health Association | Children's Home Society |

| Cosmic Turtle | Cosmic Turtle | Reflections | Co-motions |
| Vero Book Center | Back | McKee Botanica Garden | 22nd Street |

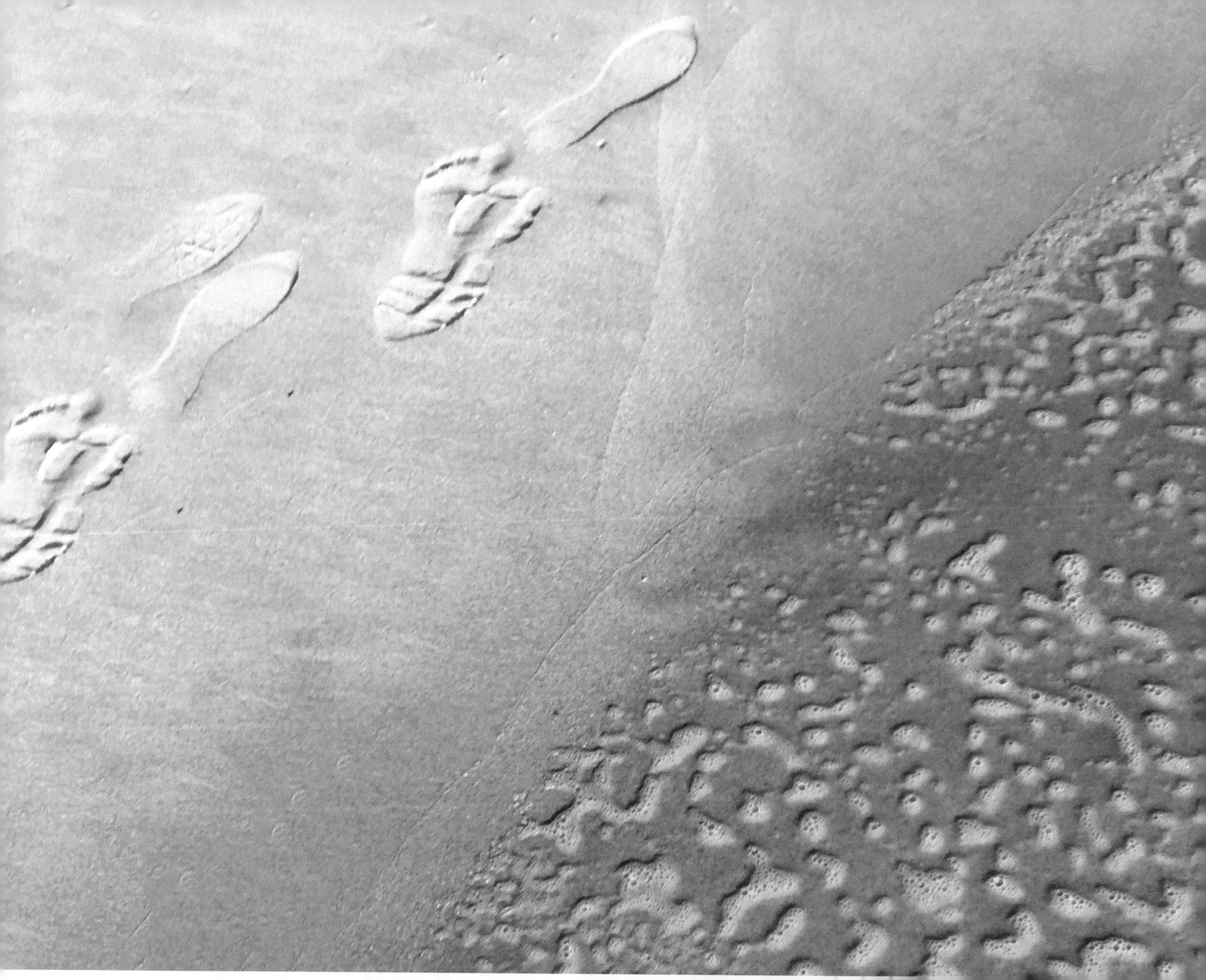

About the Author

Janet Sierzant was born in Brooklyn, New York and grew up on Long Island in North Massapequa. She moved to Georgia, where she lived there for twenty-six years. Janet graduated from Kennesaw State University with a Bachelor's Degree in International Studies and ran her husband's exhibit company, Peachtree Exhibit Service for almost ten years, and was co-owner of Escalade Indoor Rock Climbing gym with her son. She missed the beach and dreamed of moving to Florida some day. Janet finally achieved her dream. She started La Maison Publishing, Inc. and now lives in Vero Beach, where she writes books and takes daily walks on the beach.